The Road of Others

'Modern Chinese Masters' is an imprint of short fiction from contemporary Chinese writers in English translation. Each title has been chosen for its ability to surprise and challenge preconceptions about Chinese fiction.

Cover illustration by Li Zhenhui

Qingdao artist Liu Zhenhui likes to work from nature; deep inside autumn woods, watching goblins dance; or beneath branches heavy with spring rain. http://blog.sina.com.cn/liuzhenhu

The Road of Others

Three stories

by Anni Baobei

Translated by

Nicky Harman and Keiko Wong

Modern Chinese Masters

Make-Do Publishing,

Hong Kong.

English edition first published 2012.

Cover design by Gia K.

Editor: Kelly Falconer.

ISBN 978-988-18419-7-1

Contents

A Journey

I don't feel any great emotion when I look back at these works; now, they seem rather lacking but as I interrogate who I was I feel a sense of peaceful acceptance.

Life is a process that must be followed in proper sequence: we learn everything step by step; from emotion through reflection to insight. Yet on the journey of my own life, after passing time in different places, and enjoying the scenery along the way, the only thing I feel after all these trips is a feeling of emptiness.

Beauty exists everywhere, whether it be in chaos or simplicity. Sometimes beauty may reside most in the stubborn or the uninhibited, or in the modest and gentle. All these versions of beauty are aspects of a complete human nature. Compared with the views of powerful people, the words of a 'nobody' mean nothing at all. Literary works always fall short: the words put down by the writer are ultimately only connected to her own life.

But even as inadequate individuals, we may try to explore and reach a better understanding of the world around us, and try to live according to that understanding in the hope of making further progress on our journeys. Only through what we have learned along the way can we penetrate the fog of words and pass through all the controversies and changes in our lives.

Anni Baobei
February 2012

GOODBYE, AN

He didn't know where she was.

It didn't matter. She might turn up at some point. Once you started this game, it was hard not to get sucked in. He didn't know if this was down to the game itself, or because only the two of them were playing.

He'd come across her in a chatroom, he couldn't remember which day it had been. Her name had appeared as a long string of letters: V–I–V–I–A–N, an English name, but he shortened it to An. He thought it must have been a Saturday, maybe around two o'clock in the morning, when insomnia felt like a form of slow suicide.

He was listening to Paganini's *Scena Amorosa*. The music, like a very fine thread, entwined itself around his heart until the pain was so intense that he gasped for breath.

He clicked on her name and typed 'Hi'. Then he saw her answer in the red chat window: 'Hi.' Plain and casual, like his.

Him: Still awake?

An: Yup.

Him: Paganini sometimes kills me.

An: He wrote for only two strings. The other strings are to kill your thoughts with.

Him: :-)

An: :-)

And that was how it started.

They chatted for a long time. Halfway through, they took a few minutes' break. He stumbled over a chair and knocked it over as he got up to make a coffee. Waiting for the kettle to boil, he stretched his neck, his back. When it was ready, he carried the coffee back to his desk, and wrapped his fingers around the hot mug before starting again. A conversation was like a chess game: you needed an opponent; what kept it interesting was an equal match.

They carried on, their language sometimes cryptic. When it began to get light, she said she had to get some sleep. They didn't fix a time to meet again.

He went to the bathroom and took a cold shower. He craned his neck to look in the mirror. His face was void of all emotion.

He was a cold fish, he thought, afraid of only one thing – loneliness.

He took the Metro to work every morning and bought himself a coffee at the station. He'd finish it before the train pulled in. When he arrived at his destination and walked back up to street level, he'd screw up his eyes against the light. The sunlight was inhibiting, just like life itself. The road was full of the smell of dust.

Him: I'm someone who prefers the shadows.

An: I know that. Like I know you're the kind of man who goes for cotton shirts. And blue-checked handkerchiefs. You only ever wear lace-up shoes and never white socks. You don't use an electric shaver – and you use herbal aftershave. I'll bet you drink coffee as if it's water, and that you're very thin.

Him: There's something else you definitely don't know.

An: ?

Him: ?

Emerging from the Metro station, he had to cross the road and walk through a small plaza planted with cherry trees, now full of blossoms. It was the part of the city he felt the most warmth for. When he went into his office building and waited for the lift, he would tilt his head and breathe in the fragrance that lingered on his shoulders. Small pink cherry-blossom petals often clung to his jacket, and he would pick them off and chew them.

One day, in the lift, Qiao asked him: 'What do they smell like?' She worked in his company but in a different department.

He gave her a stony stare and said: 'Probably just like your lips.'

Qiao's eyes widened in surprise, then she smiled.

She was a girl who drank her water cold, liked white cotton dresses and wore trainers without socks. Her hair was very long and thick and her dark eyes shone. She didn't wear make-up. At twelve, she'd had a crush on a good-looking student in her year. By upper middle school, she'd switched her affections to Hemingway.

An: Do you know how Hemingway died?

Him: No.

An: He stuck his rifle into his mouth and pulled the trigger.

Him: Ugh.

An: He blew his skull right off.

Him: Desperate.

An: Not at all.

An: He just wanted to end it that way, that's all.

Him: You like the way he did it?

An: :-)

An: Yes. I think people should be more decisive about their lives.

An: But life has ground us down into the dirt.

Could such a girl really exist? He wasn't sure. He'd only met her online; he'd never seen her. It seemed unlikely someone that interesting could exist in real life. Her way of thinking made him wonder sometimes if she were a man. Still, she was endearing, her conversation was unusual And he liked her.

That night, when he met her again online, he said: 'Lets meet up, go to Häagen-Dazs.'

An: The one in the Isetan department store on Nanjing Road?

Him: Wherever you'd like.

He was sure they lived in the same city. As they chatted, she told him she loved the Shanghai Metro and that when she waited on the platform she often had the urge to jump down to the tracks, then scramble back up again as the train whined into the station. She liked fantasies tempered by terror, and despair.

An: Do you enjoy looking at the sea? The sea is the Earth's tear-drop, crystalline and warm.

He laughed.

Him: But Shanghai only has the Huangpu River and it's filthy!

He knew it wouldn't be easy to get her to agree to meet face to face.

For a while, he and his netizen friends would regularly meet for drinks and bowling. These friends were mostly men but sometimes there'd be women as well.

Chatrooms were the best place to get close to strangers. He'd met nearly twenty girls he'd got to know online first. With some, he'd just have a meal and never see them again. Others, like his ex-girlfriend, Lace, were different. Lace had been one of the prettiest girls he'd met this way. They'd had a feverish love affair that lasted six months. Initially, he'd felt the hunter's quick curiosity and urge to subdue her but when it was over, he thought those feelings had been cruel.

He had been silent for a long time.

He seemed to be bingeing on love.

He felt ravenous, and had to fill his empty belly. He would just ask An if they could meet. He wouldn't get his hopes up.

It was good to chat. He'd sit cross-legged and barefoot in a wicker armchair. Sometimes he'd wrap a blue patterned rug around his shoulders and over his knees. Halfway through he'd get up and make a fresh pot of coffee. Often he'd knock something over because his legs had gone to sleep.

They'd log off at dawn by counting from one to three, then at the same moment click: QUIT. He needed the few moments of warmth this gave him. It sucked him in.

He believed he was completely clear-headed when he committed himself to this virtual web world and this blur of love.

He was beginning to miss her. On his way home from work, at the Metro station, bits of their late-night conversations would come back to him: the clever devilry of her tone of voice; those sentences, sometimes cryptic and sometimes plain. He'd never met such an ice-cool girl.

Once, online, they'd talked about love.

An: Remember your first time with a girl?

Him: Yes.

An: What struck you most?

Him: The tears in her eyes, on my fingers. Their warmth.

An: Your fingers lost their virginity.

Him: :-)

An: :-)

Him: Why do you ask?

An: I want to know if there's any love left in your heart.

Him: There's about 10 percent left over. I think it's about to go rotten.

An: People who don't believe in love are more likely than ordinary people to be unhappy.

Him: What about you?

An: Sometimes my heart is full. Sometimes it's empty.

He squeezed onto the packed Metro train in the evening rush hour. As the carriage swayed along the wan lights shone on the black rails. He looked around and had the sudden feeling she might be standing right by him. She could be any one of these strangers.

The young women in the carriage were mostly office girls. They all wore suits and were exquisitely made up. He didn't think she was one of them. He had the impression she was jobless, and a drifter. Someone who liked chilling out. Besides, she normally logged on at night. If she were here, he thought, she'd spot him: a man who was protective of his lifestyle, who wore a cotton shirt and lace-up suede shoes, who had a shaved head and who smelled of herbal cologne. She was probably having a laugh in a corner of the carriage right now. She wouldn't come up to say hello. She'd just have a quiet laugh.

It was only because he'd started to pay attention to the other passengers that he eventually became aware of one particular girl. She stood on the same platform as he did every morning, waiting for the train going the other way.

For those few moments, she looked as impassive as he did, and there was a hint of laziness in her expression, too. She was dressed in black T-shirt and loose faded jeans, with strappy espadrilles on her feet. A stacked collection of silver bracelets hid her skinny wrist. Her dark hair was thick and shiny. A huge bag was slung crossways over her shoulders. Sometimes she rifled through it to pull out ear-phones, which she'd then pushed into her ears. When she listened to music, her expression became more aloof and indifferent than before.

He kept wanting to know if she was listening to Paganini. Sometimes he thought he should just go up to her and say, 'An, let's go for a coffee.' If it were her, she'd look up mischievously, then give one of her faintly malevolent smiles. If it wasn't her, she'd just turn away.

He wanted a bit more time to look at her. In his own time, calmly. He wanted to control the ending of this game.

At the weekend there was an office get-together in a nearby bar. Qiao was there, and asked him to dance. 'Do you still remember my lips?' she asked. She smiled sidelong at him in the gloom. He put his arms round her and realized she was woozy with drink. John came over and grabbed her by the arm.

'You're drunk, I'm taking you home,' he said. Everyone in the company knew that John was secretly in love with her, even though Qiao had a boyfriend who was working as a cameraman in the UK.

Qiao pushed John's hand away. 'Lin, dance with me,' she said, and leaned her drink-flushed face against his shoulder. She stared at him with bright eyes and he looked at John, standing there embarrassed. He decided to pull her out of the bar.

It was midnight by the time they made it back to her apartment block. In the tiny lift she lifted her face and asked again, 'Do you still remember my lips?'

He looked blankly at her, then suddenly pushed her up against the door and kissed her roughly.

'I haven't had sex in a long time,' she said softly. 'He's been in the UK for two years. I haven't had sex with any man.' Her lipstick had begun to run, making her lips look like torn rose petals in the gloom. There was no way he could stop himself now.

He didn't remember how many times they made love. Finally, stupefied, he fell into a deep sleep.

He woke up at her touch, and wanted her again. Her face was twisted in exquisite suffering. He could hear her pleading whispers.

He grabbed a handful of her long hair. 'Tell me you won't fall in love with me.' He knew he sounded insensitive.

Caught between shame and pleasure, she looked at him and said, 'I won't ever bother you, Lin. You're free.' Tears trickled from the corners of her eyes.

His fingers quivered slightly. In the gloom, the warmth of tears crept from his memory.

There was an accident on the Metro one evening. The train rushed into the station and a middle-aged man leapt in front of it. The squeal of brakes and a sharp cry hung in the air. Hemmed in by the jostling crowd, Lin looked at the spot where it had happened. He saw a spurt of bright-red blood. The man lay there, one pallid hand flopped open. Holding nothing.

He pushed his way through the crowd and saw the girl in black with her earphones in. She was some distance away, looking as if nothing had happened.

He walked towards the exit and suddenly felt a burning hollowness in his belly. The sunlight flooding in through the station entrance made it hard for him to open his eyes and he turned back again.

He watched calmly as the girl approached. When she was near he said, 'An, lets go for a coffee.'

She had on a black, sleeveless polo-neck; silver bracelets tinkled on her wrist. A dab of silver eye-shadow glittered at the corner of each eye – it was this summer's hot make-up look – and just below her left eye she had a pale brown 'tear-drop' mole.

She looked up at him, unsmiling. 'But my name's Vivian,' she said.

She had a slightly raspy voice, which he found calming.

He took her to the Happy Café, where he got his morning coffee. 'What would you like?' he asked.

'Cappuccino.'

He ordered an espresso, but didn't mind this slight difference between them.

'That man must be dead,' he said.

The girl ran her fingers lightly over the rim of the white china cup. 'There's nothing special about death. Maybe he'd just lost his job. Or was facing divorce. Or someone had cheated him. Or he was just tired of life.' She put her ear-phones in her bag. 'If he'd just got through that moment, he could be drinking a delicious cup of coffee.'

Vivian was a graphic designer in an advertising company. After that morning they continued to meet every now and then, usually in the Happy Café. She called him 'coffee man' because he couldn't live without his bitter, dark brew.

He found out what it was she listened to. It wasn't Paganini, it was jazz – some bass sax.

This girl was certainly unusual. Sitting over coffee with him, she would say little. Sometimes he covered her fingers with his hand. He gently stroked the flesh of her fingertips. She would look at him then with something that resembled a smile.

He took her to Häagen-Dazs. He took her to Manabe, the Japanese coffee shop in Huating Road. He took her to Time Passage, a bar that played good music. All the places he'd talked about with An online. In the dimness, the brown mole at the corner of her eye caught the light. He didn't want to kiss her casually.

She insisted that he call her Vivian. 'I don't want to be some girl in your imagination,' she said. 'Actually, you're an extraordinarily selfish man, do you know that?'

Maybe she's right, he thought. Only a selfish man could go twenty-nine years wearing cotton shirts and lace-up suede shoes. And buying 500ml bottles of Kenzo cologne. He was used to the way he felt, yet the world he lived in was way out of kilter with his dreams.

He met An online again, and thought of the pale fingers of Vivian as they rested lightly on her coffee cup.

Him: If our lives were going to end tomorrow, would you meet me?

An: No.

Him: Why not?

An: It feels like every day we keep just missing each other so we'll never ever meet up. An: Let the world keep some of its mystery. Besides, grownup games need rules.

He went to Qiao's flat a couple of times a week. If she called him.

She knew exactly how it was: they were each lonely and needy for sex. It was just till her boyfriend came back from the UK. And of course they could split up any time. She'd make him dinner. Sometimes she'd wake up in the middle of the night and watch him sleeping soundly at her side. He was handsome, his normally aloof expression warmed by sleep. Like an innocent child. She thought those moments when men were eating or sleeping were lovely, returning them to a state of sweet vulnerability.

She caressed him gently. She felt their bodies had been entangled for too long, driving their souls ever further apart.

But she had probably never had a hold over his soul.

She remembered him standing at the lift door, chewing the petals of the cherry blossom. A faint fragrance had wafted from him. He had looked dejected. Some girls loved a man only when they found him hard to understand.

Qiao was like that, and discovered she was unable to be strong-minded. She tried asking him, 'What would happen if I got pregnant?' She scrutinized his face. His eyes were cold.

'It's up to you to be careful,' he said. 'We don't want anything like that to happen.'

Qiao feebly stroked her own fingers, 'What if it did?'

He lay still, looking at her. 'Don't go making trouble. Just remember that, Vivian,' he said the name softly. She cocked her head a little, her expression gentle, questioning. On the deserted Metro platform, the high-pitched whine of the train faded into the distance. He knew they were both playing this game. Only now, the balance of power was shifting.

If Vivian acknowledged she was An, then that was who she was.

If she refused to admit it, then at least she was Vivian.

During those night-time chats, facing the screen, he was aware of the lonely sound of his fingers tapping on the keyboard. Her speech appeared sentence by sentence, then disappeared, sentence by sentence. The end could come any time.

When saying goodbye, they started to use goodnight kisses. She typed an asterisk.

When he got a cold and told her he was feeling chilly, she said, 'Have a good night's sleep, dear.' Then they hit QUIT and it was all over.

Vivian was a girl who was within his reach. At least some of his fantasies were about her. Love was just this kind of a fantasy. It meant he could forget his craving for Qiao for a time. Those shameless, ice-cold cravings.

'I want to tell you how cappuccino's made,' he said to Vivian. 'They pour dark-roast coffee into a cup, then add sugar and a big spoonful of fresh cream, and sprinkle lemon peel on top, or orange peel will do too. Then cinnamon.'

She smiled. 'You could be a barista. You're an expert.'

'After I graduated,' he said, 'what I most wanted to do was to work in a bar, mixing drinks and serving coffee.' The hours of darkness were silent, disorientating. It was a time he really liked. A pretty girl sitting alone in the corner of a bar, smoking. The mingled smells of coffee, smoke and perfume. A Paganini track playing, killing thought. A feeling of no boundaries. He could get sucked into it.

Then sleeping by day, cutting oneself off from the sunlit world.

But reality didn't permit him to chill out this way. Every day he had to cross the concrete city in the bright sunshine.

'I'm a man who likes the shadows,' he said, screwing his eyes up a little against the sunlight.

Once more the world was forcing him out naked into the light. The sun's rays could vaporize him, just like that. It was scorchingly painful. Like when, outside the lift, Qiao said she'd split up with her UK boyfriend and that she was pregnant.

All their fellow workers had been there, waiting for the lift. They knew what was going between him and Qiao. But Qiao had to shout it out and make sure they knew he was responsible for her. He had to be responsible for her. John came up to him, conflicting feelings written on his face. 'We'll be expecting those wedding bells soon then, Lin,' he said. There was laughter and banter.

He stood stock still. There was a stabbing, dizzying pain in his eyes. Amid the enforced jollity, he felt full of self-loathing.

Today was Qiao's twenty-fourth birthday.

It was an unusually dark evening. He got a tight grip on himself, stepped off the train and went up to the Happy Café for a coffee. Qiao rang his mobile.

'Come over tonight,' she said.

He was silent. Infatuation turned a woman stupid and he was tired of her stupidity already. He could hear her crying.

'If you don't come, I'll die, then you'll see!' And she hung up.

He'd never thought about getting married. This was ridiculous. Qiao had broken the rules of their game.

'I won't bother you,' she'd said. And then she'd gone and done things her way.

He began to miss An. They hadn't met online for five days. She could be anywhere. The day was going from bad to worse, he thought. Online, he would say to her: I'm unhappy, An. Then An, quietly perceptive as usual, would type a question mark. She always gave you space. She was so ice-cool, so intelligent.

That evening, he waited for her to come online, his coffee steadily growing cold. His eyelids twitched nervously. He had the feeling she wasn't going to log in. His loneliness was tearing him apart. His thoughts returned to Qiao's warm body. All he needed was her body. Not the whole of her.

At eleven o'clock he shut down his computer. He put on a cotton shirt, grey socks and lace-up suede shoes. Outside, the road was deserted under the wan streetlights. He grabbed a taxi and went straight to Qiao's flat.

The tiny lift was stuffy as usual, and reminded him of that crazy evening: Qiao's intoxicated face blooming like a rose in his palm. There was a time when they'd both been lonely and needed each other; even so, he didn't love her.

He still had 10 per cent of his love left, but it didn't belong to her.

She opened the door, the apartment pitch-dark behind her. In the gloom, they looked at each other for a few seconds. Then he closed the door behind him, and without speaking thrust her savagely up against the wall.

Why was happiness so fleeting? As he pulled out of her, he felt a sense of hopeless frustration. Just for a moment, loneliness had been banished. But there would always be despair till you could banish awareness of this world.

Afterwards, Qiao put the light on. He screwed up his eyes against the glare. 'You know I hate the light,' he said.

'We need to talk things through,' she said.

He lay back in the bed, exhausted, closing his eyes. 'There's nothing to talk about. I'm tired, I'm going to sleep.'

Stubbornly, Qiao pulled him back up to face her. Her eyes were red and puffy. She really wasn't pretty any more.

'I love you so, so much, Lin,' she said, looking at him with vacant, sorrowful eyes.

'Don't talk such rubbish! You can marry John. You can marry any man who's willing. But this is all I can give you. It's like the only thing I need from your body is this. Pardon me for being blunt...'

She said nothing more. He turned off the light and the room was pitch-dark again.

It was three o'clock in the morning when he woke. Qiao was gone. A draught blew in through the open window and the room was cold.

He turned on the light. The room was quiet and empty, but for the big black-and-white portrait of Qiao on the wall. Her boyfriend had taken it before he'd left for the UK. Qiao's pretty face wore a fragile, innocent smile. The truth was that she was different from him; not a match for him either. Only Vivian could play the game with him. Because they had the same aloof sensibility; the same patience.

Qiao was vulnerable and innocent. She needed warmth. She needed him to promise that things would last forever.

He got up to go to the bathroom but when he pushed open the door, he saw Qiao lying in a bath full of water, dark red with her blood – blood from one of her wrists. The other hung over the side of the bath, and had dripped a pool of blood onto the floor tiles. Her upturned face was still, and white, no longer blooming.

The reek of blood filled his nostrils. He bent over the toilet and was violently sick.

He left the police station for the last time and returned to the office. While he waited for the lift his head was empty of all thoughts. Exhausted, he was empty of feelings, too.

He was alone in the lift, and as it slowly ascended, he leant against the wall, shut his eyes and took a deep breath. Suddenly he heard a soft voice.

'Do you still remember my lips?' it called to him. His eyes sprang open. The lift continued to bear him upwards, swaying slightly. Cold sweat trickled down from his forehead, and over his eyelids.

'I really could not love you,' he whispered. 'I'm sorry.'

The lift door opened. All was quiet. He steadied himself and strode out.

He couldn't stay on at work. When he came out of the General Manager's office, it was to find all his colleagues standing there silently, accusingly. His face expressionless, he walked to his desk and began to get his things together. The sun scorched in through the full-length windows; he heard its fierce rays burning his face. John was blocking the doorway.

'Out of my way,' he said. John looked at him blankly but then suddenly reached out and landed a savage punch on Lin's face. Once again he smelled the sticky reek of blood.

'You bastard,' John said with enraged indignation.

He wiped away the blood dripping from his nose, moved past John, and left.

It had begun to turn cold. In the plaza, the wind blew a swathe of ochre-coloured leaves off the French plane trees. There were the usual bustling crowds. Life went on. He crossed the plaza and hurried towards the Metro station.

He went into Happy Café, and the owner greeted him with a smile.

'You haven't been in for a while,' he said. 'That girl in black's come by several times looking for you.'

A steaming cup of espresso was placed in front of him. He took a sip. No one knew what had happened to him. People flooded in and out of the Metro station every day, but they were all strangers. There was no one to talk to, no one to comfort him.

Except An. Or Vivian.

As he finished his third espresso, he saw Vivian getting off the train. She didn't notice him. She was saying goodbye to a man who seemed to be in his forties. He was ordinary-looking, though sharply dressed. He casually kissed her on the cheek before hurrying off.

She came into the café. She really did stand out from the crowd. There was something mysterious and untamed about her. Quite a woman to fantasize about.

But now he had seen through her. The truth would always out.

'Hi,' she gave a slight smile. 'I thought you'd gone for good.'

'I killed someone,' he said. 'I'm about to run away. Come with me.'

'If that's the case, I should turn you in.'

He looked at her, at her cute tear-drop mole. She looked tranquil. She could carry off that calmness better than any girl he knew. He should have met someone like this before. It would have been an extraordinary experience. Depression slowly flooded over him.

'Don't mess me around, tell me who that man was,' he said.

Her head jerked up. Her eyes were calm. 'What is it you want to know?' she asked tranquilly. 'I've never tried to mess you around. If you want to know, I'll tell you: I've been living with him for the last three years. He's married, and won't get divorced, but he gives me the kind of comforts I want in life.'

'Why can't you do that for yourself? You've got a job. You can think for yourself.'

'You think I've got the qualifications to keep myself?' She laughed bitterly. 'I have nothing. I just want to go on living like this. I don't want to be poor and I don't want to die alone.'

He said to himself, *this is absolutely normal. Absolutely. There are plenty of reasons why we desire things in this world. We don't want to be poor. We don't want to die alone.*

All the same, he felt a surge of disappointment.

'Why did you want to be with me?' he asked. He looked at the girl sitting silently over her coffee. He remembered bits of their times together. Like when he had softly touched her pale fingers. He didn't know whether they had loved each other.

'Because you came up to me to say hello that day, and I don't turn down encounters that life brings, certainly not with someone as good-looking as you.'

This game could go on. Tender yet enigmatic, giving them some relief from the tedium of their lives. But he had uncovered the truth of the matter. Like him, she liked the shadows.

'Right, I'm off,' she said. Lightly she touched his face. 'Lin, you're the millennium's loneliest coffee man. This world has no dreams for you, and there's no place for you to hide. Her silver bracelets slipped down her arm, revealing a web of red scars on her wrist. They were deep burn marks from stubbed-out cigarettes. She saw his look of shock. 'I used to do drugs,' she said. 'I've still got the scars.'

'I really don't understand you,' he said. 'I've never understood you.'

'But why do you want to understand? We've both been lonely from the start. We just need the company; we don't need to love each other.'

He didn't go home or eat dinner. He went into the nearest internet café. He would wait for An.

Suddenly he was filled with dread. An was the biggest consolation in his life but maybe she would disappear like Vivian. He waited and waited. Seven o'clock, eight o'clock, nine o'clock, ten o'clock went by. He waited online for that familiar name to pop up.

But she did not appear.

His eyes were smarting. He ordered a coffee and asked the guy who ran the café if he had any Paganini. 'I want to listen to his *Scena Amorosa.*'

'No,' said the young owner, 'I've only got U2 and The Cure.'

He said nothing more and sat back down at the computer. He wrote just one line: An, get online.

Someone wrote in his chat window: Too bad you fell in love with her, mate.

Someone else wrote: You're out of luck.

He continued to sit facing the computer, hearing the sound of rain outside. He felt empty, and remembered all those nights he'd shared with An. He'd told her about his childhood, his first love, his dysfunctional family, all the lights and shadows in his heart. No one else would ever understand him the way she did, though he didn't know who she was, or even if she really was a girl.

It was nearly two in the morning when the owner told him he was closing up.

He wanted to make a call, but hadn't brought his mobile.

'What's the number of the pay phone outside?' he asked.

Before he logged out of the chatroom, he wrote a solemn request to the others: 'Please tell the girl I was waiting for to phone me. I'll be waiting. For as long as it takes.' He typed in the kiosk phone number and her name: 'Vivian. But I call her An,' he added.

The sky was a deep blue, piled high with layers of grey cloud. He left the café and breathed in the damp, chill air of early autumn. Large drops of icy rain struck his face. He walked to a convenience store nearby and bought a pack of cigarettes and eight cans of beer. Then he went into the phone booth and waited, alone.

Every now and then a car would speed by, but there was hardly anyone left on the street. Only a carpet of yellowed plane tree leaves that had blown down in the wind. He smoked and drank his beer. It made him feel warm inside, this waiting. Almost like the comfort An had brought him. At least he didn't feel that loneliness. He even longed for it to carry on. Two hours passed. The sky was beginning to lighten. He leaned his face against the glass and wept.

Suddenly the phone rang.

He picked up the receiver. He heard a rustling at the other end of the line.

'Hello, An?'

It was a girl's voice. Clear and magnetic; the most beautiful voice he'd ever heard. She gave a little laugh. 'That's me,' she said.

He tasted the warm tears as they ran down to the corners of his mouth. They were salty. He had forgotten how salty tears were. 'An,' he said, 'I've drunk eight cans of beer in here.'

He finished his cigarette. It was raining.

'Why were you so insistent that I call you?'

'I don't know,' he said. 'I just miss you. Meet me, once, An. I don't care what you look like. You're so important to me.'

She laughed again. 'I'm not scared to see you... I'm just not in Shanghai.'

'Then I'll go and see you. Tell me where you are.'

She told him the name of the city, but not the address. 'I can't see you,' she said.

'Why not?'

'I told you before. I've been to Shanghai. I've always had an obsession with Shanghai and Shanghai men. But I'd rather keep my fantasies – you know, of you taking me to Häagen-Dazs. And to Huihai Road for a coffee. Or to a bar. That way, there's no beginning, and then there's no ending either.

'I know,' he said. 'You need the game to be perfect. But I'm not someone who can keep playing right to the end.'

'You only need one person to keep playing right to the end for this to be a perfect game,' she said.

'He watched the raindrops sliding down the glass panes. It was nearly daybreak. 'I'm leaving Shanghai soon, probably for Australia.'

'It doesn't matter where you are,' she said. 'We can always meet online. I'm here.

'Let me say one last thing,' he said.

She was silent, waiting.

He spoke into the receiver: 'Thank you for having used up the last 10 percent of my love tonight. I finally have absolutely nothing left.'

When he'd sorted out his visa, he took a day trip to the place where An said she lived.

It was a seaside city, hundreds of miles to the north. He saw the ocean, at last, which she had so often talked about online. The vast, azure ocean.

'The sea's the Earth's teardrop, crystalline and warm,' she had said. She loved looking at it.

He went for a stroll around the city's European-style, red-brick buildings with pointed roofs. There was an air of melancholy about this classical architecture. The streets were bright with crisp northern light. And everywhere were tall, slender, pretty northern girls. Perhaps she was one of those who had slipped past him, he thought.

Finally he could whisper to himself, 'Goodbye, An.'

ENDLESS AUGUST

Call me Wei Yang.

I'm a daughter of the south. Before I was 17, I lived in a southern ocean city. After that I moved to Shanghai, that metropolis of surging crowds, where the miasmic sky between the buildings looks so clean and blue, so lonely. At night a small of decay seeps across the Bund; the sad scent of materialism. Times and broken dreams are buried together and ferment, endlessly.

And the typhoon comes every year. In August.

When I was twenty-five, I told myself that I should move to the north. I didn't think they had typhoons there.

The squeal of the typhoon brings death's suffocation. It rages unpredictable and unrestrained, alive with visions. I enjoyed it, when the wind would come up, and used to play a game on the bridge near Shaanxi road: I'd stand there, lean back over the railings, hang my arms behind myself and stretch down and down. My hair would fly in the wind, I'd begin to feel dizzy, and would see the clouds flying gracefully, swiftly over the city. But I began to realize that when a girl is looking at the sky, she's not looking for anything.

She's just lonely.

I'd quit my job in a web company. And I was single.

I'd told Qiao that I know very clearly what kind of man I want. Within ten minutes of meeting someone, -- ten minutes tops -- I can tell whether or not he'll have anything to do with me. If he can bring me love, he might relieve my suffering.

Life unfolds in ten-minute segments, and I live in dread of the unforeseen. I believe that those with true intuition can't escape this fear.

Qiao was a girl I'd met in my evening English class. She was wearing a lime-green cotton jacket the colour of damp moss that survives in a cool, dark corner where the sun will never reach. A corner is somewhere that makes people feel safe, so I chose to sit beside her. Behind our books, we studied each other's palms, as if we were teenagers back in school. I liked the feeling of her hair brushing against my face when we leaned closed together.

'Your palm is so smooth, there are hardly any lines at all,' Qiao said. 'It's scary.'

'Why?'

'It means you will die young.'

'Is that so scary?'

'Maybe.' Her face seemed slightly afraid.

I smiled and massaged her fingers. A woman's skin is soft with a slight fragrance. Like petals.

After class Qiao and I would go to a bar, or just sit outside a convenience store with a plastic cup of iced Coke. She works in a design company and has a programmer boyfriend she calls Zhao Yan 'face of the morning'.

'We've known each other for ten years,' she said. 'I can only fall asleep now if I'm holding his hand.'

'Will you marry him?'

'Sure. I want to anyway. We will have ten kids.' Laughing, she rested her face innocently on my shoulder.

Smoking, silent, I smiled to myself, and watched her.

I like flowers, I like to break off the petals one by one, to mark them with my fingernails, or squeeze out their juice. I don't know why they don't have blood. Theirs is a life without pain; it's enough to make me jealous.

I was often silent, especially when I was a child. Silent children make others feel uneasy. If there are no signs of happiness when she's supposed to be happy, no tears when she ought to cry, no assurances when those are required... if there are none of these things, then she is probably one sick girl.

My mother used to sit a little apart from me and smoked as she looked at me apathetically. She was a woman with pale blue eyes and a wan, languid smile. She treated me as an adult, because she wasn't like other mothers.

First, she was desperately lonely. Second, she was a single mother. Third, she died when I was twelve.

That night was the first time I'd set eyes on Zhao Yan. He had short hair and liked to wear black shirts. He used an Ericsson mobile.

He told me why he favoured Ericsson phones: 'Because of the radiation,' he said, 'I want to get brain cancer, then the way I think about everything will be turned upside down.'

His teeth were very white, and when he smiled the corners of his lips lifted with a gentle quirk. The expression in his eyes was clear and sharp.

I laughed at what he said, and Qiao laughed, too.

The three of us would walk together around campus after class. Qiao would be in the middle of us, with her left hand cupped on my shoulder and her right hand caressing Zhao Yan's neck. Sometimes her happiness seemed fey, and I realized this concealed her lack of intuition. There was a tear-drop shaped mole at the corner of her eye. I know these dreamy indigo-eyed women; they are moss. Darkness keeps them moist, preserves in them the fragile illusion of life's sweetness.

That first night we went to a bar named 'Life'. An illusion. The patron brought over whiskey on the rocks and a pack of 555 cigarettes. Zhao Yan and I sat at the bar and watched Qiao weave like a fish through the dancing crowd.

He said, 'We've been together for ten years.'

'I know.'

'I always wonder if I can really make her happy.'

'Don't try to predict how things will turn out. Predicting the future brings doubt, and then you will be afraid.'

'You don't seem afraid.' He was studying me in the dim light.

'That's because I know some things are fated.'

'Fated?'

'Right. For example, you met Qiao; Qiao met me; then I met you.'

I smiled and raised my glass. 'Cheers, Zhao Yan.'

He tilted his head, laughed and then knocked back the remains of his drink.

The first time I went to Zhao Yan's apartment in the western district it was typhoon weather.

I wasn't really after him – I just knew there wasn't much time left. In October Qiao would very likely become his bride. But I couldn't let her leave me.

He lived in a decrepit old French-style building, a walk-up that erupted in a cacophony of creaks and cracks as we ascended the wooden stairs. In order not to alert the landlord I removed my shoes and carried them in my hand.

We sat in the dark and listened to the wind and clouds brushing against the dark sky of the city. The sound reminded me of my childhood, of the hallway to mum's room. She never hugged me or kissed me; she brought strange men home and never told me why. When I couldn't sleep I would creep barefoot along the dusty corridor to her room and listen to the groans, or else her hysterical sobbing. I would hesitate, and pace around, but finally all I could do was crouch in the corner and cover my ears. I longed for the touch of her skin against mine.

I turned and looked at Yan, and fixed my gaze on him.

He seemed nervous. 'Wei Yang, I never thought of falling in love with you.'

I smiled. 'Me, neither,' I said. 'But I know what is fated.'

He sighed. Gently he pressed his lips on my eyelids. His warm, sweet breath whispered over my face; his embrace sucked me in. From afar, I heard the unexpected noise of my shoes falling on the floor.

A pair of cotton shoes with white-ribbon laces.

I never wear high-heeled shoes.

Mother had dozens of high-heeled shoes. She arranged them in her closet, lined up rows of velvet shoes, silk ones, soft leather shoes, embroidered-cotton shoes, one pair of slim and pointy pearl-encrusted shoes that seemed to emanate coldness, and fragility. She never wore socks. Sometimes she wore the shoes inside the flat and would pace alone in the room, echoing with a lonely staccato. She was a beautiful woman, but at the time when she was most lovely the man she loved wasn't there.

She never told me what he looked like. But I know he liked her to wear high-heeled shoes. He had given her memories she couldn't forget. But no promises.

'I wanted to grab hold of something,' she laughed, 'so I had you. Then I found that I'd made a big mistake. Because you shouldn't give anything to those who don't love you back. Once you do you'll pay a heavy price.

'You are the crime I can't escape.' She would suddenly scream, lose control, and hurl her shoes at me, one after another. She would run after me, tears streaming down her face. She would be shaking with anger.

Her fury returned in cycles. She had nothing but solitude, and me. I was her only lover, enemy, rival, friend.

Finally she went mad.

Zhao Yan was sleeping like a child. When I left at midnight, I didn't kiss him.

On the street, the typhoon winds were up. Leaves were swirling around and the air seemed unusually fresh. Big white clouds flew overhead. I lit a cigarette in a sheltered niche and then let myself be swept along the empty street.

Showers of huge ice-cold rain drops assailed me, beating and stinging my face.

I sheltered in a public phonebox and rang Qiao. Her blurred voice told me she had been sleeping.

'Qiao,' I said, 'will you get married in October? The weather is really very good then.'

'Don't discuss this with me on such a windy night.' She wasn't cross that I'd woken her. She sounded amused, and pleasantly lazy.

'Men don't love women. They just need women. For example, if he's ill, then he'll demand that you see him first thing in the morning.'

'He called you then?'

'Yes, because he couldn't find you.' I exhaled a mouthful of smoke. 'I'm taking you to Beijing in September. We're going to the north, Qiao. Remember these words.'

I hung up.

It was certain that people would be looking for me the next afternoon. Zhao Yan rang first; his voice sounded tired: 'Qiao saw the bracelet on my bed. I didn't dare to tell her it was yours.'

'It's not mine,' I said. 'I never wear bracelets, she knows that.'

'She's leaving me.'

'I can't do anything, Yan.'

'Do you love me?'

'I can't agree to answer that, sorry.'

'I want you to marry me.'

I didn't say anything.

He sighed, then said, 'I know you're a loner.'

The phone gave out the sound of a broken connection. He had gone.

Qiao came to me that night. She said nothing, just curled up on my bed. She was shaking slightly. I went over to her and stroked her hair.

'Qiao, is it that painful to break up? Everything passes: people we've loved, pain, the times we live in. What's the difference?

She had her back to me, and said coldly, 'I hate cheating.'

When I was twelve I prayed that I might grow up as soon as possible so that I could control my mother, control this woman with the pale-blue eyes and wan, languid smile. I loved her. But she was insane. Her fits of throwing high-heeled shoes at me often left marks on my face. I wanted to go to school, I wanted love, I wanted someone to kiss me and caress me, I wanted to go to university, to have a job and eventually have my own family. I wanted to see the ocean, far away. I heard these unvoiced prayers shatter in my heart.

Alone in the dark I would hold a handful of petals and squeeze them with such force that the liquid came out.

Mum took one week to die. She had been walking around in her high heels and at the top of the stairs the heel broke. I saw her extend her hands, screaming, hoping to grab something to stop her fall, but she grasped out at nothing. When she reached the bottom, her head smashed against the baluster. Her blood spurted out and stained the wall, the carpet, the floorboards. In the five years after that, that blotched wall sometimes smelled of sour raw meat or fish, even after I'd spent night after night washing the wall, and crying. I kept that up until I was seventeen.

I had grown up.

I left that small southern city for Shanghai; since then, I have never once shed a tear.

Who would have believed that Yan was my first man?

I hid my blood from him. I was scared it might be blue – dark blue, the colour that reeks of solitary crimes.

No longer a little girl, I have already begun to age and wither. But in my golden period, the person I love is not with me.

Yan: I miss his body and his breath, the heat of his palm against my cool skin. No one else had ever hugged me, or kissed me. He's my only man.

September finally arrived. He rang: 'I have to go to Japan for two years, for work. If you would marry me, I would stay.'

'You've got it wrong,' I said. 'The one I love is Qiao.'

'If you want me to go, I will. If you are still single two years later, I will marry you.'

I hung up.

The typhoons passed. The autumn sky was pale and clean, the sunlight was faintly and pleasantly warm. I still wanted to go north.

Qiao looked hollow-eyed and sallow. She spent her nights getting drunk in bars and clubs and wouldn't stagger home until morning. I love these girls with indigo eyes and wan smiles; they are like my mum. Even the scent of their fingers is the same: the fragrance of petals I crushed in my palms.

I removed the high-heeled shoes from her feet and threw them out.

'My mom died from wearing these shoes,' I said. 'Because she was in love with a man, and that man loved her wearing high-heeled shoes. She became depressed because of him, and she went crazy.'

'She died?' Qiao's face was buried in her pillow.

'Yes. She had to. Life was already meaningless for her.'

'You wanted her dead?'

'I just wanted her to get rid of those shoes.' Those shoes that left marks on my face. Those shoes with no love.

Qiao embraced me. Her long hair covered my face as she sobbed. 'I know,' she said. 'I know you killed her.'

I screamed: 'I didn't! I didn't. I just wanted her to be free of her pain. Why, why, why did she have to wear those shoes?!!'

Qiao gripped my head, and pressed me against her shoulder. 'Don't be scared,' she said. 'Don't be scared, darling, I am here.' She pressed her lips to my hair.

I pushed her away. 'I don't trust you!'I pulled her hair and dragged her body to the balcony, pushed her towards the rail. When she felt her long hair flying in the wind, she cried out from fear.

'You must tell yourself that men are not reliable. You must be with me!'

Qiao sobbed. 'But I love Yan, I miss him, everyday. I want to marry him'. Her tears flew away

I released her. She knelt down, her hands covering her face.

'He loves me,' I said. 'Not you. He's going to Japan; you'll never see him again.'

It was late autumn when Zhao Yan left Shanghai. I was there to see him off.

He was standing in the crowded airport with a big rucksack and a look of abandonment on his face. He handed me his mobile. 'Keep this.'

I opened the lid of the clamshell phone to find an already yellowish photo of a sweet, smiling Qiao and Yan, hugging her from behind, his chin pressed against her ear. I closed the lid.

'She's with me now,' I said. 'You don't need to worry.'

'I'll try. You know that, Wei Yang.'

'I know.'

'Meeting you was my misfortune. You are a damaged woman – you never have time for love.

I smiled. 'But you want to marry me.'

'Yes. I want to marry you.'

'Will you still want that two years from now?'

He lowered his head, and when he lifted his face again, his eyes glistened with tears.

'Even if 200 years passed, I would still remember that night of the typhoon, the way you turned back to look at me on the stairs. You were barefoot.'

Again, I just smiled. Whether or not I am sad or happy, all I can do is smile. He hugged me. It had been a long time since I was hugged. My face was buried deep into his chest, and I heard his heart beat with renewed urgency. His breath was warm and fresh. My only man. Gone.

But I already had his baby.

I was determined to go north. With Qiao. I feared I might lose her if we stayed in Shanghai; she was wasting away day by day.

She continued to go out every night, and had even been arrested for making a drunken scene in a bar. On my lone mission to the jail to bail her out, I had to change buses several times and brave the heavy rain. I found her squatting silently in a corner. Her thick make-up was smudged, her hair disheveled, her skirt torn, and her face had cuts made by fragments of glass.

'Qiao, come home with me.'

She slowly lifted her head. 'Why do you have to be with me?'

'Because you're like my mum.'

'Your mum is dead.'

'Yes, she is. She died of loneliness, which is why I want us to be together. I want to take you away.

'You and she are one and the same. I loved her, Qiao, do you understand? She was my only friend. My only lover.'

'But why do you have to choose me?' She pushed me; her face was full of tears.

'Because this is fate, Qiao. It's fate which can't be avoided.'

'Do you think you can control me?' She laughed coldly.

She riled me, and I replied. 'I can control you, Qiao, let's be clear about that. I can control everything about you.'

Her face to the wall, she broke down into hysterical sobs.

I had booked us on an evening flight. Shanghai to Beijing.

Qiao and I were in the departure lounge. My bump was visible now, and I'd had to foresake my jeans. For our flight, I had chosen a light-pink, thick cloth skirt. I had already found a place to live and a job. I would also continue to write. And there was Qiao. The person I loved.

That day she had on that same lime-green jacket she had worn the first time we met.

She was wearing lipstick. It seemed a long time since she had taken this much care with her appearance. I actually preferred the natural look on her, but for her this was a new beginning. She knew that now that Zhao Yan had gone, that I was the only one she could rely on.

'Wei Yang, look how many people there are!'

'Yes. Lots of people who don't know each other.'

'So what if they know each other? They will still have to part.'

'But the people we have known leave something in our lives, especially those we know well. We won't forget them.

Qiao didn't react. She said she wanted to go to the washroom, and transferred her earphones to my ears. Before she got up, she looked at me.

'Wei Yang, Why did we sit together that day in class?'

'Because you wore this pale green jacket. I liked it.' I patted her cheek.

'Wei Yang, do you love me?'

'Yes, I love you.'

'Zhao Yan said he loved me, too, but later he didn't love me anymore.'

'That's because love changes as time passes. That's the way things are, unless time stops.'

She nodded, and then smiled widely and brightly. 'Good. It won't take long,' she said, and then sprang up and away from me.

She was the girl I liked, moist and cool like moss. Free. I rested my hand on my belly; it had become a favourite posture. I still hadn't told her I was pregnant but I thought when I did that she'd be pleased. This would be our child.

The music coming from the earphones was from Tanya Chua, the singer she liked, singing in a subdued tone: *He has already changed, you can sense his new lover, then you finally know, that person you loved has gone, before you have even said goodbye. Our heart's longing is only for a memory, of who once was.*

The song was on a loop, and Tanya Chua's voice kept singing to me for ages. I lost track of time. Suddenly though I saw chaos unfold; many people were running, and there were cops. I pulled out the earphones, and dragged our heavy duffel bag along behind me to see what was going on. Qiao really should come back and help me, I thought. It was getting close to departure time – and if she didn't come back soon we might miss the plane.

The crowd seemed to be most swollen at the entrance to the washrooms. I dove in and a man's elbow jabbed my belly. I started to scream hysterically: 'Let me through! Let me through! Let me in!' I left the bag, and charged in. A woman was lying still on the white tiles. Her limegreen jacket was soaked with blood. The inside of her wrists slashed red and maw-like. She was barefoot, her shoes nowhere in sight. Her eyes hadn't had time to close. She was dead.

I never went to the north. I decided to pass the winter in the south because I wanted the birth of my child to go smoothly, because I was alone again: Qiao had found a way to leave me.

I kept thinking of our first meeting, our heads down behind our books, looking at our hands. Her hair was pitch black and fragrant, her eyes a dreamy blue. She had believed in love. I loved everything about her; the one I loved.

Zhao Yan wrote to me:

My life goes smoothly in Tokyo. It is only at night when I can't sleep that I hear the wind and clouds screaming, mixed with Qiao's tears. If there was no you, Wei Yang, I would probably have married Qiao, and lived a normal life with her in Shanghai. So many times I ask myself, why was it this way? But if I had to choose again, I would do the same again. How are you, Wei Yang? How is Qiao?

I didn't reply. My belly grew day by day. I have no fear of anything in life, because there is nothing I fear to lose, and nothing I terribly desire. If there had once been something, I suppose it was love, but now I felt safer without that.

I didn't want to forget anyone though. I thought of mother, how she paced the floor in her high-heeled shoes. Like a friend she had showed me all her loneliness and despair. And there was Qiao, whose happiness was unrestrained by fear or any sense of self-protection. Once, her happiness had filled me with hope, that with her I could find peace. Then there was Zhao Yan, my only man, who gave me a child.

I wanted to see them every day, so that I could mould my child to their likeness. But all I had was the small picture of Zhao Yan and Qiao he had taped on to his Ericsson, the yellowish and blurred photo that was now starting to peel away. For ages I would stare at those faces broken and beaten by both pain and happiness.

Then one day, that small photo was somehow lost. Zhao Yan and Qiao's faces were gone, leaving their outlines only in my memory.

The Shanghai winter was very cold that year.

At night when I slept I felt dread in my bones. The people I loved, one after another had gone, one after another had left me. I had mimicked my mother's method to catch a life. But I thought that, unlike her, I wouldn't have any regrets.

In the dark I shut my eyes, thinking about Yan's soft lips, gently touching my eyes. I softly said his name out loud.

One week before I was due to give birth, I called him.

His voice was warm and clear as before. His manner was unexpectedly friendly.

'Zhao Yan,' I said, 'I think I should be honest with you about a few things: one, as a child, I killed my mother; two, I deliberately wanted to split you and Qiao up; three, Qiao killed herself in the airport washroom, she is dead. If you are still willing to talk to me, I will tell you the rest.

There was a long pause at the other end of the line. No sound but Zhao Yan's breathing. My iPlayer was playing Tanya Chua's song, *He has already changed, you can sense his new lover, then you finally know, that person you loved has gone, before you have even said goodbye. Our heart's longing is only for a memory, of who once was.* Finally I knew how deeply she had loved him, but at the time she had said little, and done nothing. She was a petal I had squeezed in my fingers, squeezing her life into my soul. When she died in an airport full of strangers, she had taken off her shoes. She had gone barefoot.

My laugh startled the connection, and then I listened carefully to the silence at the other end. I heard a soft crack. Zhao Yan had hung up.

When the child was newly born, her eyes were bright with indigo fires. She was an exceedingly beautiful girl with pitch-black hair damply clinging to her head. I wanted to take her to the overpass on Shaanxi Road. I wanted to embrace her, lean backwards from the railing, and slowly face upwards, let my hair fly in the wind.

The clouds formed themselves exquisitely in the sky, spreading across the city.

As she slowly grew up, she would understand: when a woman looks at the sky, she is not looking for anything.

She is just lonely.

I stayed on in the south. Qiao and Zhao Yan belonged to this city. And so did my child.

I sent Zhao Yan letters. I didn't know what I could write, so I sent him blank sheets of paper, sometimes stained with tears. In a tiny rented house in the north-west corner of Shanghai I began to write again, and made enough to support myself and my child. If time continued to flow, I thought fate would work itself out.

Spring arrived. I continued to study English two days a week. I took the child with me, and coaxed her into sleeping while I was there.

If she cried during class I would take her outside and hold her as I walked a circuit of the dark playground. The playground had many oriental cherry trees whose powder-white flowers floated like soft raindrops in the wind. I put the petals in the child's hand, and she gripped them and smiled.

My deskmate was a thirty-year-old woman with short, spiky hair. She liked to wear clean white shirts. Once, she came over to me and offered me a smoke, for which I felt very grateful. She favoured a masculine scent from Kenzo, which suited her clean appearance, and made me happy.

She said, 'Your baby is beautiful.'

I smiled. 'Because she looks like the person I love.'

She nodded. 'You are lucky.'

'Yes. I always think so.'

'You can call me Jo.'

'Hello, Jo.'

She sat with me in the shadow of the cherry tree. We smoked, and looked at the blossoms fluttering around us. The child made indistinct murmurs in her sleep. Jo's hand reached out, and gently caressed the child's hair.

At that moment, I thought of Qiao. I thought of that night we had drunk iced coke outside that convenience store. It was already a long time ago.

But the happiness was endless.

THE ROAD OF OTHERS

It was raining.

As I listened to the rhythm of the downpour, I felt as if I'd passed through a long dark tunnel to the exit from a dream. It was as if a new cycle of life were unfolding. Dusk, pale and blurry as water powder, entered through a slit of curtains.

Bald trees, spires of neo-classical villas, silent streets: the city was sinking into soundless chaos.

I realized I was alone in a white-washed room. Soft sofa, floor-lamp, a white rug, lush ferns. This wasn't my room.

Sam was back.

I chose randomly from the rail of cotton shirts in his closet. The shirts were all white. In the small adjacent bathroom, as I took a shower, hot water washed over my hair and streamed down my face. My brain was rapidly revived.

This was the first time Sam had taken me home but it was exactly like I'd always imagined it would be: everything was white. Simple and clean, dustless. No female clutter, no flowers. Nothing fancy. Nothing lusty. Just a clinical place. I had been right, there were no women in Sam's life; he was just an older man who ran a bar and liked to polish his wine glasses.

The only personal touch in his bedroom was a picture in a silver frame; a black-and-white print, yellowed by age. It showed a young boy with a sweet smile, probably a European. He was casually dressed in torn old jeans and a clean shirt and was sitting by a fountain in a square. The glare of sunlight caught by the camera already seemed to belong to the past.

Sams neat shirt flapped around my dirty jeans as I descended to the first floor and approached its owner across a white wool rug. On the third floor I had passed another bedroom and a study. On the middle floor a sitting room and kitchen. He had made the first floor into his bar. Sam was asleep there on the sofa bathed in a pale light seeping through the pulled-down white linen blind. Sam's bare feet were up on one end of the sofa and his head was on a cushion at the other.

All I could hear in that sealed box was the rhythm of the rain.

I stood by him and lit a cigarette.

Being in this room was like sitting at the bottom of the ocean. The clamour of the rain seemed unreal. I took a drag on the cigarette while

I looked at this man and the lines on his face, the track-marks of passing time. How handsome he would have been when he was younger. When I pressed my lips gently to his fingers I felt his blood flowing there. His eyes opened.

'Why am I here?'

'I called you from the airport but no one answered,' he told me. 'Your keys were in the door, you phone was off, your windows open. You were lying in bed with a fever, wine bottles and cigarette ends everywhere. You've never known how to take care of yourself. You're risking your health.'

'So do you feel sympathy for me?'

'Do you need my sympathy?' He looked at me calmly. 'Why have you been silent for so long?'

'Some difficulties at home. And I finished my novel.'

'I've read it,' he said. 'Was everything OK while I was away? Have you caused any trouble, or lost anything?'

'I got married. And I travelled in Xinjiang.'

'Married?' He looked at me skeptically. 'But you still live alone?'

'My man scarpered, with our marriage certificate and another woman.'

He touched my head. 'Qiao, why do you keep making the same mistakes?'

'No idea. Never tried to figure that out.'

'How was Xinjiang?'

'Cramped, the same as everywhere.' I started drift around ten years ago. We all struggle senselessly, like fish in a tank.

I want to visit a small island in Taiwan. On the east coast.'

'Why?'

'I want to see the sea in winter, with you.'

His eyes showed signs of affection as he looked at me. He touched my hair again.

'Why did you have it cut?'

'I'm starting my new life.'

We took the ship to the island.

The whole trip took about ten hours and we had to spend a night on board. The ship was empty. Not many people go to sea in winter. The island only became busy with tourists during the summer.

Sam said, 'The first time you came to my bar you walked in with this vacant look, as if you were escaping the world. You ordered a drink, unzipped your jacket and revealed your crumpled black cotton top. I had a feeling then that you were different.

'How different?' I'm just as fickle as anyone. Lusty for life, easy to break.

I drew on my cigarette as I leaned against the balcony railing. For the moment I was actually tranquil. Travel always brings me peace. Maybe it's because people usually feel hopeful when they head for a new place.

After a long thrilling whistle, the ship departed at around 9pm. It sailed east though the Huangpu River and the night. Blurred florid neon lights flowed on the river like paint poured in water. Fading and fading. Perishing. The vast and magnificent city was slipping away behind us. Finally it dissolved in the shadows of night.

I said, 'This boat will pass my hometown.'

'Do you miss it?'

'No,' I said. 'I just want to take a glance when we pass. Only a glance, mind.'

A storm got up on the broad river. The ship began to pitch. Looking out through the door of our first-class cabin we had a partial view of the forward deck. There were just the two of us. Sen shut all the windows and the doors and then tucked me in my quilt.

'There's a gale outside,' he said. 'Stay in, have a good sleep.'

I lay on the bed. During the course of the night, the tide surged. At midnight, Sen came over to my bed. His light breathing inhabited the dark. I kept silent, and my eyes closed. He leaned over me and straightened my blanket, then he sat on a chair.

'Can't you sleep?'

'No,' he said. 'Neither can you.'

'I was afraid I would miss it if I fell asleep.'

'Is it close now?'

'Very. What did you dream of most often when you were a child?

'A face beside me in the dark. Looking at me.'

'Like now?'

'Yes.'

As the ship passed my hometown only the peaceful harbour could be seen. It was dark, and the outlines of buildings looked fuzzy, obscured by pale lights on the bank. I leaned over the railing to watch and the cold wind pierced my shivering body to the bone. Sen stood quietly beside me.

'What's it like?' he asked.

'A typical east-coast city. Typhoons every summer. Tall parasol trees along the street. A vulgar city full of vulgar people, although plenty of celebrities have come from there, because people raised there are stubborn. They are smart, due to the seafood.'

'Why did you leave?'

'I just followed my instinct. It told me to go far away.'

'Never to return again home again?'

'There's no place for me there now. I've got used to living with my own soul.

Cities. Cities are caves where histories and memories, happiness and sickness, lust and sex are buried. Cities are paths that extend endlessly through time, without destination.

I fell asleep again. In my dream I was holding a man's hand and his fingers were like water moistening my skin. My heart seeded a silent longing, tears welled in my eyes. The man's face became indistinct.

Sen placed his hand on my eyes. The warm tears slid down my cheeks.

I can't remember when this started, that I sometimes begin to cry for no reason. My tears have nothing to do with sadness, are unrelated to happiness. There's just this warm salty water that comes out of my eye sockets and then slides down my cheeks, leaving a faint trail as it dries. Actually, I don't think of myself as a melancholy girl; being in tears is just a physical phenomenon, like people burping when they are stuffed. My tears are worthless whether there are too many or when I remain meanly dry faced.

We arrived at the island that afternoon, struck a bargain with a minibus driver, then climbed into his dilapidated vehicle. The island air was refreshingly cool and with a slight brackish smell of the sea. There weren't many tourists, just stark trees as far as the eye could see. We got off the bus when we reached a cliff above a beach with soft sands. The sea was muddy, the tide raging and the wind piercingly cold.

We walked on to the village and found our guest house. Our room was on the second floor. It was a simple set-up: four single beds in a room; thermos on a bedside table; a quilt with a pattern of broken flowers. The landlord had already prepared our supper of potatoes, rice noodles, snakefish and cabbage.

'It's not the food you're used to,' I said, 'but this is what we east-coast people eat everyday.

'Let's take a walk on the beach after dinner.'

It was freezing by the sea.

In the pale moonlight a winding, grey sand path extended to the depths of the dark woods far away. A flight of stony stairs led us to the beach, where the roar of the sea filled our ears. There wasn't a soul around but empty, silent shadows advanced towards us across the sand.

'The first time I came here was for a high school spring outing. We slept in the temple, and we could hear our footsteps echo on the floors of the wooden rooms. At night, I sat on the rocks by the sea and once, there was a huge downpour. I ran back to bed and lay there listening to my classmates walking up and down the corridor and having fun. Outside my window was the rhythm of the rain and sound of trees swaying. I felt a connection with this place. I knew then that one day I would bring someone back and that we'd sit here until the sun rose.'

'Who says we can stay here until the sun comes up? It's too cold. You'll get sick.'

'I know. Sometimes life can't be as we would like it to be.'

We sat on the rock and watched the deep night of the sea. In front of us was boundless dark water, swelling in the moonlight. You couldn't make out the horizon. After several tries, I lit a cigarette, protecting the light from the wind with my hands. I realised my hands and body were trembling. In the dark my cigarette end would flare up and then the light would fade. My hair was flying across my face.

'Hold me, Sam,' I said in a low voice. He held me against his chest. His dark overcoat had the scent of his cologne. 'What are you thinking?

'About something in your book. When you wrote that many people are living in quiet despair and never even realize it, so the end of their stories doesn't matter.'

The violent roar of the surging tide and the freezing wind swallowed our voices. Dark is eternal and infinite, an irresistible force.

After three days on the island, we were ready to go back to Shanghai.

On the way back I developed a fever. Unable to move around, I lay on my bed. A headache and dizziness combined with the rolling of the ship made me very sick, and I couldn't stop vomiting. Sam didn't sleep, and took care of me all night. His warm hands held me tightly as I began to murmur incoherently.

In the middle of the night he helped me take some pills. My cold sweat finally broke.

'Qiao your health is not good. You get sick too easily.'

'Maybe I'm too susceptible.'

'You've been murmuring the name of the character in your novel. You have been living in the world of your novel for too long, it's time to finish it.'

'It is finished.'

'Sometimes I really worry about you,' he said. 'There's a darkness in you.'

'Have you seen it?'

'I know you. Not understand, not know about; just know.

'Everyone must keep going, whichever way they can. Sometimes though, there's a bit too much despair. Life is a seed blown in the wind, lost in the vast wilderness of time. There for just a moment, then it's vanished.

I smiled at him. 'Sam, why is that I don't feel as if we're heading back to Shanghai. We seem to be going somewhere else, far away.'

He walked out and smoked a cigarette in a freezing gale. I had never seen him smoke before. When he came back to the room he said, 'Qiao, would you like to go to the UK with me?'

As I looked at him, he seemed very calm.

'I suppose everyone's guessed long ago about me,' he continued. 'The only man I've ever loved was French. He died in a plane crash seven years ago. I was in London, he was in Paris. He caught the shuttle each week, then one day he was gone. I couldn't stay in London – too many memories. So I returned to Shanghai. By then I was thirty.

'My parents both stayed in the UK and, even though I'm far away from them, they keep asking when I'm going to get married. Because I have never told them the truth.

'This time I'm going back because my dad is dying. He doesn't have long left. My mom keeps hinting that I should realize his dream for me while he's still here.' Sam looked straight at me. 'Go to the UK with me,' he said. 'I'll tell them that we're married. After that we can come back, set up home in any city you like. We can live together, enjoy our freedom and take care of each other.'

'Which means you can never love me.'

'Do you want that, Qiao?' he said. 'What you want is a flower growing on the other side of the river. Blossoming in an unreachable place…'

Back home there were messages on the answerphone from Little Zhi, my best friend. Her voice seemed slightly unfamiliar after all this time but still sweet.

'Qiao,' she said, 'I'm still in Kathmandu. I like it here. I'm working in bar run by an American. He's going to close it after three months and go to Africa. The Dutch man is gone, too, so I watch the sunset alone. Come visit me when you have time; I'll be here for three months.'

And there was my ex, ZhuoYang. His voice had also become strange. His message said: 'Qiao I want to see you, could you please call me back.'

I hesitated before deciding to meet him. I had a foreboding it would be another parting. I was sure that he had loved me once, that at some moment of time it had been the true feeling.

I waited for him in the lobby of his flashy office building in Huaihai Road and watched him emerge from the lift. He was wearing a formal suit and it seemed that he'd become a real office man. His shoes gleamed. He was no longer the fresh boy in a black T-shirt, and I struggled to recollect the slight grassy scent of his skin. We age this way: struggling from one end of time to another.

'Qiao,' he nodded at me. 'You had your hair cut.'

'Ugly, isn't it?'

'You're always good looking in my eyes.'

I laughed with my discovery that he was still the Shanghai man with a childish sweet temper. He didn't dodge me when I leaned to kiss his cheeks. He said, 'I'm going away next week. To France.'

'It's all arranged?'

'Yes.' He explained. 'Life has made me numb. If there's no change, life is just like death.

'Open a video store when you are old and make sure it is stocked with great movies.'

He forced a smile. 'I may not come back. I'm going with Yang Lan, she likes France. She wants to settle down there.'

'Are you two married?'

'Soon.'

'Keep an eye on her, don't let happiness slip away.'

'I can't prevent that. Lots of things happen that we don't expect.'

He kept looking at me but his eyes appeared tired. We went to a cafe for coffee.

'Is Little Zhi ever coming back?'

'Probably not. She's ignorant about herself, never knows what she wants. It's best for her to lead a drifting life in this way.'

'What about you, how will you live now? I heard that a wealthy man was chasing you.'

I laughed. 'No. No way. No such luck.'

I couldn't tell him that Sam could offer me anything I wanted. Except love. There was no perfection.

He gazed at me and said, 'Qiao you are still the same. Melancholy but never deterred. At this moment I really, really want you.

'ZhuoYang,' I interrupted. 'Let the past rest undisturbed. I'm not someone with luck, I drive away happiness.'

'Have you finished writing the movie script? Are you going to give it to that director?'

'No, I don't think he'd do a good job.'

'Why did you write it then?'

'Because...' I smiled. 'Because I needed to show it to... someone. Write the movie, take it to an empty cinema. Empty, waiting for a stranger to arrive. Then play it for him.'

'And then?'

'Then the audience leaves.'

'Are you leaving Shanghai?' He suddenly met my eyes again as he asked this.

'Yes. Can't find a reason to stay here.'

'Will I never see you again, Qiao?' He held his gaze.

'Why should you? Many people don't meet again. We're all just passing through. Forgetting is the best way for us to respect what we had.'

I returned to my place to pack. There was way too much junk: clothes, furniture, books, perfume bottles, plants. No way was I going to take any of this with me; it's best not to clutter your life. Our possessions also have a relationship of destiny with us, and when the time comes we shouldn't be afraid to shed them. Without taking too much care I put my laptop into the bag, some favorite books and CDs, then a few clothes. Then I called my landlord.

'I've paid all the bills. You can keep the deposit and furniture and other junk I left.'

'Didn't you say that you'd stay for two years? You've only been here a few months.'

'It's long enough.'

'Are you leaving Shanghai?'

'Yes.'

'Will you be back?'

'Probably not; it's not my home.' I smiled to myself.

But where was my hometown? Anyway, if I'd ever had one I couldn't go back there any more: a hometown is somewhere you can't go back to.

In my suitcase was a sheet of newspaper a homeless person had given me. It was an interview with a Beijing man teaching in an isolated village. The man had turned his back on city life and in the interview he said:

We reach the same place by different routes. I've wanted to teach since I was very young. Children are flowers from paradise, untouched by dust. Life has only this short period of innocence. Just look at their faces.

Our lives have lost touch with our ideals. We are always busy with other things...

At the corner of the street I stopped to light a cigarette. After that, I bought a cup of Japanese fish balls by the entrance to the subway. I joined other transients at the wooden counter to eat them. The crowd of passengers emerging from the trains swelled like a great tide behind us. This was the Shanghai where I had stayed for two years. Sunlight moved through the small gaps between the high buildings. People rushed by through the blue sky. This was the city I had known. Its brilliance and its low side. Its countless flirtations. I had never known any other city as ice-cool or brilliant as Shanghai. If you looked down from the top of one its many towering skyscrapers you'd see that the city was a magician's conjuring trick – it could vanish anytime, suddenly. A magnificent mirage.

The solitude of the city was that of the ocean. You could sink to the bottom, soundless.

I walked into the subway. As the carriage rumbled forward underground, I found that I was surrounded by a group of people who were also going to the railway station. They talked loudly about shopping, about where they'd been, what they'd bought. Many people had come here just for shopping. But I had lived here. I wrote, I met up with strangers, and now I was leaving.

All my departures felt the same.

I closed my eyes and, feeling dizzy in the crowded subway car, imagined standing alone on a mountain peak. The hot sun blazed onto me, clouds moved past with the moaning wind and I heard a faint sound of dust flying away from my heart. It suddenly became clear: I knew where I should go.

Just like I knew why I had come to this city.

I bought the ticket. There was half an hour more until departure. I browsed at a store near the station and bought a bottle of water and two newspapers. Then I saw the phone booth on the street, walked in, dialled the number.

'Sam, it's me.'

'I've been waiting for you to call.'

'I have wiped everything I wrote from my computer.'

'Where are you?'His voice became quiet. 'Are you leaving?'

'Yes. This movie is over. The audience is drifting away. You should leave, too.'

'I know,' he said.

'Sam, this coin? It's yours. I used it to make this phone call.'

'What about my proposal?'

'I think I love you, Sam, so I can't accept a way of being with you without love. I'm sorry.'

'I need you, Qiao. Don't go.'

I smiled. 'Sam, the one thing I feel grateful to heaven for is that you came to the island with me, and gave me the chance to play you the movie in my heart. Because you were the only one qualified to be my audience.'

'Are we never going to meet again?'

'If one day I come back and your bar is still there, I'll go in and have a whiskey on the rocks.

Your cocktails are very good – they always get me there.'

'Where are you?'

'Somewhere. I'm tired, Sam. I have to stop this movie now, find somewhere and someone I can settle down with, take a break.'

'Can you find them?'

'I think so.' I smiled again. 'Anyway, I'll keep searching; we both will. If you travel to another bank and look back at the road you had been walking on, it seems different.'

Sam's sad voice stayed in my ear after I hung up. He'd still had something to say. But everything had frozen, and he was too late. All that had happened while we had briefly waited for each other suddenly dissolved.

I walked out of the phone booth, my bag in my arms, just as the snow came. Once again, I was immersed in an endless stream of strangers. Once again I found that losing your own past, memory, feelings, and home was just like being reborn. It rescued me from emptiness and freed me to travel through time to the emptiness of another place. Shadows flashed before me; those who had got close to me or touched me, those whom I had hugged, whom I poured out my heart to, those who had sat with me and looked at the flower on the other bank. Their souls were the rocks that had helped guide me across the river. Together we had shared a brief stage of our journeys.

At the end of the street, I stood and watched the first snowflakes of this Shanghai winter. I held out my palm; icy snow melted there. In my more than twenty years of life, snow had always been the same. It was something eternal that would never change.

A blurry shadow of a man suddenly appeared on the other side of the road. He was wearing a blue tunic, his hair was blowing everywhere, and I realized I had been waiting for him endlessly. For someone who was destined to leave me. It made me sure that there must be someone, somewhere, who was waiting for me on the other bank.

We were standing on opposite ends of emptiness, alone.

My eyes were warm with tears. I watched. The man's shadow vanished.

At this moment, I finally found my peace and happiness.

I wrapped my coat tight around me, picked up my bag, and walked through the now heavily falling snow towards the station lights in the depth of night. It was time to leave.

SEEKING AN

Our search begins in Shanghai, 1998, at the brink of a new millennium. China had only about five million people online, less than 5 per cent of its population. Deng Xiaoping, whose 1991 'Southern Tour' kick-started China's long march into the capitalist era, had died only the previous year.

Into this protean cyber-historical space, enigmatic stories under the moniker Anni Baobei started to appear on a website called 'Under the Banyan Tree' (*Rongshuxia*). They were strange tales of individual emotion, desire, suicide, sex, death, escape, and had a compelling effect on their readers, many of whom appeared to desire some kind of personal connection with her. Indeed, one of Anni's fans blogged about falling asleep with her head on the print edition of the stories, her heart full of raging emotions.

Anni Baobei rapidly became a sensation.

There was much debate about what kind of person Anni Baobei could be. Despite her alias, which to Chinese readers sounded exotically

Western, people were unsure whether, in the words of one of her own characters, 'such an ice-cool girl could really exist'. Noone knew where she was, and there was speculation that Anni Baobei might not be a woman at all.

Anni did eventually reveal herself, and for a time would appear at events hosted by Rongshxia. A few details became known – such as her real name, Li Jie, and the fact that she, like her character Qiao of 'The Road of Others', was from an east-coast city. Similar to the fashionable white collar-ites of her online stories, Li Jie lived in Shanghai and had worked in advertising, and for a magazine.

These sketchy details enhanced Anni Baobei's image as a guide to an emerging world where self expression could be realized through consumption. Shanghai in the late 1990s appeared to many young Chinese as a world full of alluring possibilities. A new capitalist ethos of individual gratification was taking root, but still had to contend with the communist-era hangover collectivism, and asceticism. After a lengthy hiatus, the city had resumed the role in had played in the 1920s as the first point of contact with the West, symbolized by its Bund waterfront of colonial-era architecture. Western fashions and consumer goods were enthusiastically seen as representative of a new sensibility of personal expression.

The characters of Anni's early stories are in many ways icons for this brave new world of conspicuous consumption. Her characters wear clean white shirts and Kenzo perfume, they never drink 'ordinary' coffee but always 'exotic' choices such as cappuccino or espresso; they hang out in bars with names like 'Time Passage' and 'LIFE', and consume Häagen-Daz ice-cream in fashionable stores on Nanjing road. The characters are, or aspire to be, Westernised: they attend English classes; they have boyfriends who work in the UK.

This concern with surfaces led Anni to be referred to as a 'Xiaozi' (petty bourgeois), a label that had at one time been a lethal political condemnation but which by the late 1990s had become more ambiguous. Part of her appeal to the younger generation was that she appeared to offer herself as a guide to this new domain of individual expressivity through consumption.

Unlike other novels of that era which appear to celebrate China's nascent consumerism, Baobei's early stories, although displaying a fascination with the possibilities of consumption as a new language of self-expression, are also tempered by a lingering sense of opposition. 'Endless August' opens with a description of the sense of decay seeping across the Bund and 'the sad scent of materialism'.

Anni seems to have been aware that the consumerist lifestyle was (and in many ways remains) an unattainable fantasy for most young Chinese: the expensive world of chic coffee bars, gleaming department stores and trendy bars she describes was in truth beyond the reach of many. Her readers may have been living in modern cities but most still had to accommodate the traditional values of their parents. At work, they faced structures that were still hierarchical and patriarchal and concepts such as sexual freedom were regarded suspiciously by the older generation. The appeal of Anni's fantasies of individual freedom may partly be explained by their contrast with the actuality of the regimented, constrained lives of the majority of white-collar workers (*bai ling*.)

2

After her brief moment of exposure, Anni soon disappeared again, this time for good. From the release of the print version of 'Goodbye, An' (*Gaobie Wei An*) in 2001, she has refused to make any public appearances. Her relationship with her readers can be compared to that of Vivian (Wei An) and of Lin in 'Goodbye, An', whereby on the one hand there is a willingness by her readers to imagine a personal relationship with her and on the other there remains a writer who insists unfailingly that her readers know her only through her words.

Over the past ten years, Anni's fiction has evolved from the passionate and dark-edged early stories to her more ruminative mature works. Her readers have appeared willing to follow her. Nearly every one of her many books has been a bestseller in China, selling from six hundred thousand to over one million copies each. She was one of China's best-selling writers during that period, in any genre, and now holds a uniquely respected place in Chinese literature. Her complete works were recently reissued in a tenth anniversary edition and she is regularly invited to join overseas-bound delegations of China's top writers.

Anni Baobei's writing, with its focus on individual desire, expressivity and subjectivity, represents a culmination of a trend in Chinese fiction that began in the 1980s with literary movements such as the *Fansi* ('introspection') school, the *Shanghen* ('wound') school and the *Gaige* ('reform') schools, whose members exercised greater, though still circumscribed, freedom of expression. Leading writers of the period – such as Ma Jian, Yu Hua, Su Tong, Ge Fei – didn't want to write 'politicized propaganda works.' A further step in this direction came with the 'individualism' school of writing of the 1990s, notable for its association with female writers, especially Chen Ran.

Anni's works can be seen as an expansion of this subjective individualism into cyberspace, where she took advantage of this new medium's possibilities for solipsistic retreat. Pioneer netizens usually found at internet cafés or sitting at their desks at work – few at that time could afford their own computer. This new world-wide-web allowed them to venture into a previously restricted realm of the senses, and to escape from the demand of collective social responsibility. The internet appeared as an eroticized space full of the allure of the other. Anni's stories inhabited this space, and their popularity soon led her to be described alongside Li Xunhuan and Ning Caishen as one of the 'three chariots' of early online Chinese literature and a forerunner of slightly later web-based sensations such as Murong Xuecun.

Anni has been referred to as a feminist, despite her instinct to avoid such labels; nevertheless, many of her books are concerned with the private female experience, an alternative point of view to an often macho Chinese writing scene that subordinates female characters under the male gaze. In contrast, Anni's female characters are not concerned about their gender, nor do they allow themselves to be limited by it: they fearlessly search for the fulfillment of their desires, including sexual desires, they believe in the validity of their feelings, and that they can control their fate. The characters became icons to a generation of young

Chinese women struggling to re-identify themselves in a changing world.

Even so, Anni's female characters reflect archetypes of Chinese femininity. The delicate, idealistic Qiao, who commits suicide in two separate stories, or the ice-cool Vivian can been seen as incarnations of different aspects of Lin Daiyu, the moody heroine of 'The Story of the Stone' whose highly refined sensibility appeared to lead inevitably to her early death. The image of the fragile woman is a common one in Baobei's work: in 'The Road of Others' Qiao is seen to be unable to look after herself and too easily falls ill.

More broadly though, Anni's stories explore the limits of the illusion of individual expression and remark upon solitude, death, loneliness, parting: the price of freedom. In 'Goodbye, An' the character Lin's fantasies in cyberspace cannot be realized, they lead to disaster in the online and offline worlds, and to his abandonment. The stories are suffused with the threat of 'the unforeseen'.

The stories of 'The Road of Others' are woven with such themes, unified by the various manifestations of a character called Qiao, a Chinese transliteration of the English name 'Jo'; the themes and this character add to the sense of a philosophic investigation underlying the often dark and sometimes bizarre plots.

The highly personal feel of Anni's writing has encouraged readers to look for the 'real An' in her works. An (the same Chinese character as the first character of Anni Baobei) is the name Lin gives to the 'ice-cool' girl he meets online and this encourages us to make this identification with the author; in 'Endless August' Qiao refers to her hometown as an east-coast city, and it is easy to assume that this may in fact be Ningbo, Li Jie's home town. But it is 'The Road of Others' that appears the most temptingly autobiographical – it was originally the third segment of novel in three segments called 'The Road to Elsewhere': in the first segment, Qiao is a young writer struggling to live in Shanghai as she completes her novel; the second segment is Qiao's novel; the third and aforementioned 'The Road of Others' tells what happens after Qiao completes the novel.

Anni has repeatedly cautioned her readers against making too direct an identification between herself and her characters. Yet she continues to play the game: her later works such as 'Lotus' and 'Spring Banquet', also include characters who might be thought of as similar to her.

3

Anni Baobei's later novels are often set outside city boundaries, and are concerned with spiritual, emotional and physical journeys. 'Lotus' (2006) is about Qing Zhao, a young woman suffering from a terminal illness. She travels to the grasslands of the Tibetan plateau to await death and when she arrives she meets Sheng Sheng, a middle-aged man who has retired there from the rat race. Qing Zhao and Sheng Sheng embark on a journey up the Yalazangbu river gorge; along the way he recounts the story of his long-lost friend, Zhao Nei, whom he has been looking for. The twists and turns of their physical journey mirror their spiritual progress towards self understanding.

Anni's later novels and stories make it clear that her underlying interest is in spiritual freedom rather than material culture *per se*. This focus soon led her away from the themes of cities and materialism, which in her early stories exist in a piquant tension.

The later works also see the evolution of a new style; less spontaneous and without the dark pessimism that shades her earlier stories. These later works are more philosophically mature, engaged with nature, and often draw on themes from ancient classical literature. However, these characteristics, although less prominent, are also present in the early stories. For example, nature intrudes on the Shanghai of the early stories with Wei Yang's rapturous embrace of the typhoon, with the drifting cherry blossoms, the darkness of the sea, the rhythm of the rain and the fleeting chill of snow; 'Ba Yue Wei Yang', the Chinese title of her short story 'Endless August' is a quote from the *I Ching* (Book of Changes).

Over time, Anni Baobei's work has come to stand for a unique and exquisite aesthetic of individuality and creativity, in opposition to the formulaic, mundane and ugly impulses of industrial society and the crassness of consumerism. In 'Lotus' she describes a pond of lotuses as a metaphor for a range of spiritual conditions: 'some full flowering and unconventional, some sucked down in the silt, submerged by the water, some close to flowering but needing more light.'

Anni Baobei continues to prefer mostly to keep her distance from her readers and yet in an early scene of *Spring Banquet* (2011), her main character, a writer, receives a letter from a Chinese woman in her thirties who is married to an Australian and living in Australia. The letter describes how ten years previously, on her way to start a new life abroad, the woman had bought a copy of one of the writer's early story collections and spent the ten-hour flight reading it. She had no expectation of a reply but had simply wanted to tell the writer how the stories had given her courage, and how they continued to be important to her.

This scene could perhaps be seen as a gesture of appreciation from the 'ice-cool girl' to her readers, and an oblique invitation for both writer and readers to continue their separate but parallel journeys on the road to elsewhere.

About the Translators

Nicky Harman lives in the UK. She has worked as a literary translator for a dozen years and, until the spring of 2011, also lectured at Imperial College, London. She led the Chinese-English group at the British Centre for Literary Translation Summer School from 2009 to 2011 and in 2011 was Translator-in-Residence at the London Free Word Centre. Authors she has translated include Zhang Ling ("Gold Mountain Blues"), Yan Geling ("Flowers of War"), Han Dong ("A Phone Call from Dalian: Collected Poems", and "Banished! A Novel") Hong Ying ("K-The Art of Love") and Xinran.

Keiko Wong hails from the south of China and is currently living in Beijing. While reading for her computer science major at the Beijing Institute o Technology she discovered that her real passion was for writing and photography. Her English stories have been published on the Make-Do Studios website while other Chinese authors she has translated include Wu Sumei. Keiko's work can be found at www.imnotblue.com.

<u>Modern Chinese Masters</u>

Yu Li: Confessions of an Elevator Operator

by Jimmy Qi

Biting satire...Beneath the humour, serious issues simmer. Time Out

Hilarious fiction...eye-catching and thought-provoking. Global Times

Yu Li is an inspector at a fake wine distillery in a small town without any tall buildings in Hebei province. After he is fired for drinking the wine during his inspections, Yu Li manages to land another job as an elevator operator in a luxury apartment building in the far-off capital, Beijing.

The apartment building is home to the winners in the new China: celebrities, the new rich, and big-shot officials. Misadventures abound as Yu Li struggles to adjust to the confusion of city life and above all to subdue the 'nuclear weapon' in his pants.

ISBN: 978-988-18419-1-9

Make-Do Publishing

I Love My Mum

by Chen Xiwo

One of contemporary China's most outspoken voices on freedom of expression for writers. Asia Sentinel

I Love My Mum is a shocking tale of murder and incest and a powerful metaphor for corruption in modern Chinese society. The story is narrated by a hardened vice squad detective who is used to the seamy side of life. But even he has never come across a murder case like this. And the same is guaranteed for the reader.

ISBN: 978-988-18419-2-6

Make-Do Publishing

The Magician of 1919

by Li Er

Li Er pushes at literary boundaries in his work, which often experiments with narrative form. South China Morning Post.

In 1919, the year of the May 4th movement in China, magician Bigshot Cowrie arrives in Peking. He has with him a budgerigar, which is a language genius, a hat with a magical long queue and some pigeons. During his time in Peking, he encounters various figures, fictional and historical, and becomes involved in important events in modern Chinese history.

Li Er is widely acclaimed as one of China's most innovative writers, on a par with the likes of Mo Yan, Yu Hua and Su Tong. The Magician of 1919, translated by Jane Weizhen Pan and Martin Merz, is the first of his works to be published in English.

ISBN: 978-988-18419-6-4

Make-Do Publishing